AN M. NIGHT SHYAMALAN FILM

THE LAST AIRBENDER

TRIAL BY FIRE

by Michael Teitelbaum
based on the series *Avatar: The Last Airbender* created by
Michael Dante DiMartino and Bryan Konietzko
based on the screenplay written by M. Night Shyamalan

Simon Spotlight
New York   London   Toronto   Sydney

SIMON SPOTLIGHT

An imprint of Simon & Schuster Children's Publishing Division

1230 Avenue of the Americas, New York, New York 10020

© 2010 Paramount Pictures. All rights reserved. *The Last Airbender* and all related titles, logos, and

characters are trademarks of Viacom International Inc.

All rights reserved, including the right of reproduction in whole or in part in any form.

SIMON SPOTLIGHT and colophon are registered trademarks of Simon & Schuster, Inc.

For information about special discounts for bulk purchases, please contact Simon & Schuster Special Sales at

1-866-506-1949 or business@simonandschuster.com.

Manufactured in the United States of America 0410 COM

First Edition 10 9 8 7 6 5 4 3 2

ISBN 978-1-4424-0290-4

0710 UMG

CHAPTER 1

My name is Zuko. I am the prince of the Fire Nation. We are a proud and strong people who have been taught that fire is the strongest of the four elements—stronger than air, earth, and water. It is our destiny to rule the world.

One hundred years ago a plan was put into motion to allow the Fire Nation to assume control over the other three nations—the Water Tribes, the Earth Kingdom, and the Air Nomads. There was only one person who could stop us from achieving our goal, and that was the Avatar.

In every generation the spirit of the Avatar is

reborn into a new person, a bender from one of the four nations. Benders are people who can control their native element—air, water, earth, or fire. I, myself, am a powerful firebender. But only the Avatar can bend all four elements.

When it was time for the Avatar to be reborn a century ago, the leaders of the Fire Nation knew that he or she would be reborn as an airbender. And so my forefathers destroyed all of the airbenders in order to end the existence of the Avatar.

During all this time no one has seen the Avatar. Most people believed that the Avatar was never reborn. But my father, Fire Lord Ozai, ruler of the Fire Nation, believes that the Avatar may still live.

And so do I. In fact, the existence of the Avatar is my only hope.

Recently, my father banished me from my homeland and stripped me of my honor. I spoke out of turn to a Fire Nation general in defense of some friends who were about to be sacrificed in battle. As punishment, I had to fight a duel—with my own father. The scar on my face, at the hand of my father, is the outward sign of my humiliation. But the pain runs much deeper inside. I have lost my home, my honor, and the respect that a Fire Nation prince deserves.

My father told me that the only way I could restore my honor was to capture and bring the Avatar back to the Fire Nation. Then I would be welcomed home and maybe even finally earn my father's love.

And so I search. Others have searched for many years with no luck. But I have not given up hope. I believe the Avatar still lives. He or she would be quite elderly by now, but that is not unusual for one of such great power.

Many months ago I set out on a voyage aboard a Fire Nation warship to search the world for the Avatar. I stopped in cities and villages in all the nations, looking for clues, anything that might lead me in the right direction. Some days I felt hope. Other days, nothing but despair. Still, I knew that I had to continue. I had no other choice.

One morning, as the sun rose high into the sky, I stood on the deck of my ship, gazing out at the horizon. As I peered out at the churning blue sea, I suddenly spotted a brilliant white light shooting up into the sky. It looked like a glowing column rising from the ground and disappearing into the clouds.

I had never seen anything like that. No force in the world that I knew of could make such a light. I grew hopeful. Could this be the sign I had been searching for? I could not afford to leave any clue unexplored. I had to find out.

Dashing down to the lower deck, I looked over our navigational maps and realized where the light was coming from.

"Navigator!" I cried out. "Set our course for the Southern Water Tribe!"

CHAPTER 2

As we approached the Southern Water Tribe the air grew frigid and the ocean turned to ice. My ship's strong metal hull smashed right through the ice, and soon we reached a dock at the edge of a village.

"Soldiers, firebenders, follow me!" I ordered as a metal platform slammed down from the ship onto the icy ground.

I led my troops into the center of the village, which was nothing more than a collection of igloos sitting in an ice valley.

What weak people these are, I thought as I marched through. Old men, women, and children

had gathered outside. Some bowed respectfully, as they should. Others cowered in fear. These were not warriors. They were simple village folk who would put up no resistance.

"I am Prince Zuko, son of Fire Lord Ozai and heir to the throne of the Fire Nation," I told them boldly. "Bring me all of your elderly."

No one moved.

"Very well, if you will not bring them to me, my soldiers will," I shouted, turning to my troops. "Search every igloo!"

My soldiers went from igloo to igloo pulling out all the old people and gathering them in a group before me. To my surprise, among the prisoners was a boy in a cloak. He carried a tall staff and could not have been more than twelve or thirteen years old.

"Why have you brought me this child?" I demanded, annoyed at this waste of my time.

"Look under his cloak, Prince Zuko," a soldier replied, pushing the boy toward me.

"You're scaring these people!" the boy exclaimed.

"That's the point," I replied, then reached out and lifted the hood of his cloak. Odd-shaped tattoos ran across his bald head. I recognized the tattoos from pictures. They were the tattoos of an airbender!

But how could that be? We had wiped out all the airbenders years ago. Even if he were an airbender, he could not be the Avatar. He was a mere boy.

"Who are you?" I asked, releasing his cloak and staring hard at him. He definitely was not a Water Tribe villager. "What's your name?"

"I don't need to tell you anything," the boy said defiantly.

"Firebenders!" I called out. Five of my best fire-benders immediately surrounded the boy. Then I told the boy, "I am taking you to my ship. And if you don't come, I'll burn down this village."

I waited a moment as the boy looked around at the villagers. Then he spoke in a low, defeated voice. "I'll go with you," he said. "Don't hurt anyone."

I nodded at my soldiers, who grabbed the boy and shoved him in the direction of the ship. Just before I turned to leave, I spotted a boy and girl rushing forward. My best firebender kicked out, pulling flames from a nearby cooking fire and sending them racing just above the heads of the two foolish children.

"Stay back!" the firebender shouted. "Or the next blast will be lower."

The boy and girl stopped. They now knew, as so many others have learned, that it is pointless to defy the power of the Fire Nation.

I turned toward the dock, and followed the troops back onto my ship. I will discover who this mysterious boy is. Uncle will help me learn the truth, and perhaps my quest will finally come to an end.

CHAPTER 3

"Prince Zuko, did you find the source of that light?" Uncle Iroh asked as I stepped back aboard my ship.

My uncle is a well-mannered, caring man who smiles and laughs often—too often, I believe, given our situation. I must admit, though, he has always been good to me, ever since I was a young boy. And now that my father has rejected and banished me, Uncle has taken it upon himself to support me on my quest. He is and always has been, in every way, more of a father to me than my real father ever was. I trust him and follow his advice. In truth, I don't know where I'd be without him.

Uncle, too, is an outcast of sorts. Once a great Fire Nation general and a powerful firebender, he failed to capture the Earth Kingdom capital, Ba Sing Se, during a huge battle. He left the army, broken and humiliated. He also lost his own beloved son in that battle. And so I have become his son, and he my father—two rejects traveling the world, looking for redemption and a way to restore our honor. Perhaps my way has just come aboard the ship.

"I found this boy, Uncle," I said, pulling off the boy's hood. "I think maybe we should perform the test on him, despite his age. What do you think?"

"It could not hurt," Uncle said, eyeing the boy's tattoos. "And it will reveal the truth, as it always does. Bring him to the prison room."

Once we were in the room the boy demanded, "What do you want with me?"

"I'm going to perform a little test on you," Uncle explained in a gentle tone. He is kind, even to this stranger who may be our greatest enemy.

The boy looked at him suspiciously. "What kind of test?" he asked.

"Oh, I assure you it won't hurt," Uncle promised. "I've performed it hundreds of times. It will only take a few moments, then you are free to go."

The boy stared at both of us.

"Would you mind if I put a few things in front of you at this table?" Uncle asked, pointing to a small table in the center of the room. "It will only take a moment."

"That's all you want?" the boy asked.

"My name is Iroh, and you have my word," Uncle replied.

The boy nodded, then took a seat at the table.

Uncle walked to a corner of the room and returned with a tray filled with several items. He placed the tray on the table across from the seated boy.

Reaching out toward a small candle on the tray, Uncle lit it. The flame flickered wildly. He then picked up the candle and set it down in front of the boy. The flame immediately stopped moving. It stood atop the candle, straight and tall, completely still.

He had passed the first test. But that proved nothing. So have others.

Uncle moved his hand slightly and the flame vanished, sending a thin curl of smoke rising into the air. Placing the candle back onto the tray, he next picked up a small jug of water and slowly poured out a small amount onto the table close to the boy.

I watched in amazement as the water, moving on its own, reformed itself into a perfect circle. It held its shape firmly right in front of the boy. Uncle stared at him. I could see that he too was surprised by the results.

My excitement grew. Two of three tests completed and passed. Only one more to go and then, maybe, I had indeed found the long-lost Avatar.

Uncle took a cloth and wiped up the puddle of

water, then reached for the final object on the tray—a long, thin rock. He placed the rock on its narrow edge on the table in front of the boy and let go. It should have fallen over as it did every time Uncle performed this test.

But in front of this mysterious boy, the rock stayed balanced on its thin end, defying gravity and confirming what I had hoped to be true. Uncle turned and looked at me. I could see the excitement in his eyes. I felt the same exhilaration. It was true. We had found him. My long search for the Avatar was over.

I stepped up to the table. "You are my prisoner, boy," I declared. "I'm taking you back to the Fire Nation." At last my honor would be restored.

The boy looked up at Uncle, his eyes full of confusion at the betrayal. "But you said I would be free to—"

"I apologize," Uncle said, clearly shaken. He was a man of his word and I knew that he was upset at having to go back on a promise.

But I did not care.

"I should have explained further," Uncle continued. "If you had failed the test, as all others have, then you would have been free to leave. But as it turns out, you are the only one in the entire world who could pass this test." Uncle paused and bowed his head. "It is truly an honor to be in your presence."

Enough! Sometimes Uncle is too patient, too polite. The only honor I'm interested in is my own. And now that I have succeeded where so many others have failed, that honor will finally be restored.

CHAPTER 4

I stared the Avatar straight in the eyes.

"Don't even try to escape," I told the boy firmly.

It is hard for me to accept that this mere child is the Avatar. Still, the evidence is clear.

"This is a warship," I continued. "This room is made entirely of impregnable metal. There are armed guards outside this room, and my uncle and I are expert firebenders, so—"

The boy moved with startling speed, jumping up onto his chair, stepping on the table, off my shoulder, and over my head. I was stunned by his swiftness and the way he moved, almost weightlessly, floating through the air. He truly was an airbender, as his tattoos had indicated. I thought we had eliminated all the airbenders. Obviously, I was wrong.

"Stop!" I cried, spinning around to see him land behind me. "There's no way you can escape."

He brought his hands together, then pushed them forward, palms out. A fierce wind rushed through the room, forcing the door open. Then reversing this move, he created another blast of air that lifted him off the ground and pulled him out through the doorway, slamming the door shut behind him.

Uncle and I looked at each other, stunned by the speed and power of this child. The Avatar had been reborn, after all.

Grabbing the door and throwing it open, I dashed out into the hallway in time to see the Avatar slam my guards against the wall with a gust of wind.

He grabbed his tall staff and headed up the stairs toward the deck.

Following him up and out onto the deck, I saw that the Avatar was already surrounded by my soldiers. Ha! How foolish of him to think he could escape.

But just as I stepped toward him, I heard a deep wailing sound echoing off the sheer ice cliffs.

The boy looked up and I followed his gaze to see a large white creature, a bison by the look of it, standing on a high ice ridge just ahead of the ship. Seated on the beast were the boy and girl from the Water Tribe who had tried to interfere when I took the Avatar from their village.

"Don't move!" I ordered. "You have nowhere to run."

The Avatar shook his staff and wings popped out on either side. He started running full speed toward the edge of the deck—then just kept on going, leaping off the ship.

I raced to the railing, expecting to see a splash as he plunged into the icy water. But the splash never came.

"He's gone," I cried. "Where did he go?"

"There," said Uncle, who had just joined me on deck. He pointed to the sky.

Looking up I saw the Avatar flying on his winged staff, soaring up toward the flying bison, who waited and bellowed from the nearby cliff.

Disappointment and humiliation, all-too-familiar feelings, rushed through me. I felt my uncle's hand on my shoulder, trying to comfort me as he always did. Often he succeeded. But this time—this time was different.

"You found the Avatar, the bridge to the spirit world," he said softly. "You actually found him, Zuko."

He was right, and part of me knew I should be pleased. He could usually help me find some posi-

tive in a bad situation. But right now no words could bring me comfort. "I underestimated him because he looked like a boy," I said. "I won't do that again. I had him, Uncle. For a moment I had my honor back."

"It's not by chance that for generations people have been searching for him and you were the one to see that light and find him," Uncle said. "Your destinies are tied together, Zuko. That I can be sure of."

Uncle's words made sense, but they did not remove the bitter sting of failure. I looked up and saw the bison jump from the cliff and fly off into the sky, carrying the Avatar and his friends.

"But what I'd like to know is—where has he been for a hundred years?" Uncle asked when they had disappeared from view.

CHAPTER 5

We set out to sea, hoping to pick up the Avatar's trail, trying to figure out his next move. I charted a course in the direction we had seen the bison fly, and hoped to find some clue that might lead us to him.

One afternoon, several days into our chase, I spotted another Fire Nation warship approaching us. It was much larger than mine. When the ship got close enough, I recognized Commander Zhao, leader of the Fire Nation navy, standing on its deck.

The commander is an arrogant, fierce-looking man who seems to enjoy his role a little too much. He is certainly not someone I trust.

"Prince Zuko," Zhao called out. "Would you and General Iroh be kind enough to join us for lunch aboard my ship?"

What did he want? Zhao had long been a close confidant of my father's, and he had never shown me much respect, even before my banishment. I warily agreed, and Uncle and I soon found ourselves in the mess hall of Zhao's enormous ship. We were seated beside Zhao at the head table. Hundreds of soldiers sat at long tables eating and joking easily with one another. I ate my food slowly, my guard up.

Commander Zhao stood and the hall went silent. "I wanted to thank the great General Iroh and the young Prince Zuko for dining with us," he began. "I remember watching Prince Zuko playing with all the little girls when he was a boy."

My stomach started to churn. My body tensed up. So this was why he invited us: to humiliate me.

Zhao continued, "As you all know, the Fire Lord banished his son, Prince Zuko, and renounced his love for him. He will not let Prince Zuko return to the throne unless he finds the Avatar."

The commander bent over and looked under the table. "Wait, Prince Zuko," he said mockingly. "I think I see the Avatar. He's been hiding under this table for one hundred years. No wonder you couldn't find him."

"I have found him!" I shouted out.

The mess hall burst into a wave of scornful laughter. I felt every eye in the room on me. I wanted to run.

I wanted to blast Zhao with a firebending strike. I wanted to be anywhere but here.

Zhao looked at me and spoke again, his voice now deadly serious. "The Avatar was killed in the raid of the Air Nomads and was never reborn," he said, snarling disrespectfully. "And yet you continue to cling to the lie that he still lives."

My hands began to tremble. The impulse to destroy this arrogant fool with one swift firebending move was overwhelming. I noticed the flames on candles all around the room bent toward me. This firebending action was completely involuntary, the result of my building rage. Uncle placed his hand on mine, offering me silent guidance. I took a deep breath to calm myself and the candles returned to normal.

Zhao turned back to his men. "You may ask, 'Why would his honorable and wise father send his son on such an impossible task when the whole of the Fire Nation has searched for a hundred years and found nothing?' Well, sometimes children need to be taught lessons because they don't know how to behave. I commend the Fire Lord's discipline. For example, it seems I need to remind Prince Zuko that during his banishment, he is considered an enemy of the Fire Nation and is not allowed to wear the Fire Nation uniform."

Everyone stared at my uniform. My discomfort grew and the rage within began bubbling back up.

"But we will let him wear it today," Zhao said, "like a child in a costume."

I could not stand the humiliation any longer. I pushed my chair back and jumped to my feet. "One day my father will take me back!" I whispered angrily to Zhao. "And you will bow before me." Then I turned and ran from the mess hall.

I pushed past several guards on deck, then scrambled down the ladder, back onto my own ship. A few minutes later, as I stood on deck, trying to forget Zhao's words, Uncle walked up and stood beside me. He knew I was in no mood to be comforted and so he remained silent, but he was there for me nonetheless.

I turned to him, frustrated and ashamed. "We have to hunt down the Avatar, Uncle," I said firmly. "We must find him before anyone else finds him first."

CHAPTER 6

Picking up the Avatar's trail, we tracked him as he moved north through the Earth Kingdom. In a Fire Nation colony set up in the Earth Kingdom, Uncle and I stopped in a tea shop for a cup of tea.

Uncle and his tea. The only thing he loves more than good food is hot jasmine tea. I can take it or leave it, but to Uncle, drinking tea is as essential as breathing.

"We're close, Uncle," I said, joining him at a small table in the tea shop, keeping my face and scar hidden. My spirits had improved since the nightmare aboard Zhao's ship. We were getting closer to the

Avatar and his friends. Soon I would have him. "They've been moving farther and farther north. We're catching up to them."

Uncle sipped his tea. "There are a lot of pretty girls in this town, Zuko," he said. "You could fall in love here. We could settle down, and you could have a blessed life." Then he leaned toward me and added, "We don't have to continue this chase."

Uncle is a smart man, but sometimes he just doesn't understand. I know he is only looking out for me, offering me what he views as an easy way out. But living with this shame could never be easy. "I'll show you why we must continue, Uncle," I said, spotting a Fire Nation child.

"Hey, little one, come here," I called out to the boy. When he came over, I told him, "You look like a very smart boy. What can you tell me about the prince, the Fire Lord's son?"

"He did something wrong," the boy replied.

Everyone knows the story, even small children. There is no end to this humiliation.

"He spoke out of turn to a general in defense of some of his friends who were going to be sacrificed in a battle," I explained. Could this child possibly understand why I did what I did?

"Then Prince Zuko was sentenced to an Agni-Ki duel," the boy went on. "But when he showed up, it was his father he was to fight."

"That's right," I said, old emotions stirring within me.

"He would not fight his father," the boy continued.

"No, he would not," I said, fury rising in my throat. "His father mocked him and said, 'I should bring your sister up here to beat you.'" I can still see his face and feel the deep shame of that moment.

"Then the father burned his son to teach him a lesson," the boy concluded.

He recited this story as if it were a history lesson

in a book. The entire Fire Nation must believe my father did the right thing. This only serves to make me feel worse—much worse.

"How would you feel if you were Prince Zuko?" I asked him.

"Ashamed," the child replied without hesitation.

"Why?"

"Because I would have no honor," the boy said before running off.

I am right. Everyone, even children, knows that I have been stripped of my honor. And I know there is only one way to get it back.

I turned to Uncle and pointed at the retreating boy. "And that is why we must catch the Avatar first," I whispered. "Then we can think about pretty girls."

Uncle reluctantly agreed and we continued our journey.

Several days later I learned that Commander Zhao had captured the Avatar and was holding him at the Northern Air Temple, a sacred place to the airbenders.

My worst fears had been realized. My greatest adversary, the man who had humiliated me by claiming that the Avatar was dead, not only knew that he was really alive, but knew where to find him—and had captured him before I did.

But perhaps he had really done me a favor. I could now recapture the Avatar myself. I knew that I could not fight my way into the temple against Zhao and his soldiers. I needed secrecy and deception to slip in, grab the Avatar, and get back out again. But I could not tell Uncle my plan. He would only object or tell me it was too dangerous.

I put on the black uniform of a firebender and strapped my swords onto my back. I would remain hidden in the shadows, moving like a spirit through the darkness. To hide my face, I wore an old spirit mask, painted blue with an evil grin designed to frighten those who saw it. Now with renewed determination, I hurried to the Northern Air Temple. I was no longer Prince Zuko; I was the Blue Spirit.

When I arrived, I spotted a bridge leading right to the temple. A locked gate on the bridge was guarded by Zhao's soldiers. I saw a huge Fire Nation war machine roll up to the gate.

It was time for the Blue Spirit to make his move.

As the gate swung open, I slipped under the

giant machine and clung to its underside. When it had rolled across the bridge, I dropped off the machine and climbed up to the top of the temple's high wall. Peering down into the courtyard I saw Zhao addressing his troops.

"I am sending a personal message to the Fire Lord informing him that the once-feared Avatar is our prisoner and no threat to our might," Zhao announced.

I smiled beneath my mask, imagining the expression on my father's face when he learns that the Avatar has been taken from right under Zhao's nose.

I crept into the temple and ambushed several guards. Then pulling out some rope I had brought, I tied the unconscious guards by their hands and lined them up. This was a little message for my good friend Commander Zhao from the Blue Spirit.

Moving silently down the hall, keeping to the shadows, I found the room where the Avatar was being held. I opened the door slowly and stepped inside.

CHAPTER 7

Once inside the prison room I saw the Avatar hanging by his hands, dangling from a chain that hung from the ceiling. His eyes opened wide when he saw me.

"Who are you?" he asked nervously.

There will be plenty of time to reveal my true identity once you are safely my prisoner, I thought, but I said nothing to him.

Reaching back over my shoulder, I pulled two silver swords from their casings. The Avatar's expression turned to fright.

"Wait, don't!" he cried.

I raised my swords. He closed his eyes. Then I

swung the swords, slashing at the chains, slicing their metal loops open. The Avatar dropped to the ground and opened his eyes, shocked to realize he was still alive.

Moving swiftly to the door, I pulled it open then waved my hand, signaling him to follow me. I slipped back out into the hallway with the Avatar close behind.

Good. He trusts me. Once I have freed him from this prison, he will gratefully follow me. And then he will be mine.

Just then footsteps sounded from around a bend in the hallway. I pushed the Avatar back into a corner and we crouched there together, cloaked in the shadows. From where we hid I could see the guards I had tied up earlier.

Zhao and several of his guards came around the bend.

"Send word to the Fire Lord that once again I have accomplished what he has asked me to do without any incident," Zhao said. Then he caught sight of his unconscious men.

"Fools," he snarled in frustration.

Again, I smiled under my mask.

When Zhao and his men had hurried away, I ran to a stairwell and dashed up the stairs with the Avatar following. As we ran I heard a guard shouting.

"Close the inner gate!" he cried. "The Avatar has escaped. Seal him in."

Emerging out into the temple's courtyard we found ourselves surrounded by Fire Nation guards. Almost instinctively, as if we had been comrades in battle before, the Avatar and I split up, moving to opposite sides of the courtyard.

I was immediately confronted by four firebenders. Whipping out my swords, I deflected their fire blasts with my blades. Then, glancing back over my shoulder, I saw the Avatar leaping past the guards,

airbending himself away from the temple.

No! He's escaping. I set him free and now I'm going to lose him again.

Suddenly five more firebenders approached me. I continued to deflect their blasts, but as their numbers grew I found it harder and harder to fend them off.

Not only had I lost the Avatar, but now I was going to be Zhao's prisoner as well.

Then, from out of nowhere, the Avatar landed between me and the firebenders. He unleashed an airbending blast that knocked half of them over. The others shot fire at him, but I stepped in front and knocked the flames away with my sword.

Zhao shoved his way through the crowd and stood before us.

"Do not kill the Avatar!" he ordered, and immediately the Fire Nation soldiers stopped attacking. "He will just be reborn again."

So Zhao doesn't want the Avatar dead. Here's my chance to complete this mission after all. To Zhao's surprise, I pushed the Avatar in front of me and held my blade against his throat.

"Why are you doing this?" the commander asked, trying to peer inside my mask. "Who are you?"

Then it was my turn to be surprised. Zhao suddenly shouted, "Open the gates. Let them out."

I didn't know why he was letting us go, but I wasn't going to stay around to find out. With my sword still pressed against the Avatar, I led him quickly across the bridge and away from the temple. As I prodded him forward I heard a whistling sound coming from behind.

Turning back, I

barely had time to see an arrow speeding through the air. It struck my mask . . . and then everything went dark.

I awoke slowly to find that I was at a campsite in a forest. The Avatar must have carried me to safety after Zhao's archers shot at me.

The Avatar . . . I looked around, and he was whisking himself up into a tree!

I fired a blast at the boy, determined not to let him escape. But he only leaped to a higher treetop and disappeared into the forest.

I tried to get up, but I was too unsteady, and quickly collapsed to the ground. The Avatar had escaped! I had failed—once again.

CHAPTER 8

After resting for a while I struggled back up to my feet and made my way through the forest. I had to get back to the ship, where Uncle would be waiting for me and worrying about where I'd been.

I trudged through the wooded area, my body aching and my spirit once again battered. How many times had I had the Avatar in my grasp and how many times had he slipped away? Was I destined to never capture him? Destined to remain the banished prince forever?

I could not accept the quiet life Uncle wanted for me, hidden away somewhere, knowing that I had lost my honor. My name would always be spoken with laughter or scorn. There was nothing else I could do but continue my pursuit. Someday, somehow, I would capture the Avatar and fulfill my destiny as the heir to the throne of the Fire Nation.

After many hours of hiking, I stepped from the dense forest thicket out into a clearing at the bank of a large river. There I found Uncle doing his firebending exercises. He looked relieved to see me.

"Zhao's men have been searching the coast," he explained. "They were looking for you. I told them you were on a vacation with a girl. They were on our ship, searching it."

I glanced out to see the ship anchored offshore.

"Where have you been for four days, Zuko?" Uncle asked urgently.

"Nowhere," I muttered. I did not want or need to share the details of my latest failure. Uncle would only try to comfort me, or worse, try again to convince me to give up my quest. It was time to resume our search.

"We have to keep moving," I said, heading to the ship. "The Avatar is traveling again."

"Take some rest first," Uncle suggested. "You

look like you've been through a great deal. When you wake, we'll have tea together and then start the engines and get on our way."

He did have a point. I was battered and drained. A few hours of sleep would give me the strength I needed to continue the journey. I headed back toward the ship, where I stretched out on my cot, closed my eyes, and tried to fall asleep.

But my mind kept replaying the events at the temple, as I tried to figure out what I could have done differently. I hated to admit that this boy is a clever adversary, even if he is the Avatar. He moves with the legendary quickness and trickiness that airbenders were always known for. I had to rethink my strategy. Next time I would have—

A hissing sound made me leap suddenly from my cot. I caught a whiff of gas, and immediately started running as fast as my weary legs would take me. I dashed back up on deck, desperately trying to get off the ship before—

KA-THOOM!

The entire ship erupted in a massive explosion.

CHAPTER 9

Just as the ship exploded I dove off the deck and plunged into the water. While flaming debris crashed down all around, I held my breath and remained underwater until nothing more fell.

Swimming to shore, I found Uncle sitting on a log with his face buried in his hands.

"Zuko!" he cried when he saw me. "You are alive." Uncle wiped the tears from his face.

"I jumped off the ship just in time," I said, dropping to the ground to catch my breath. "This was no accident, Uncle."

"No, it was not," he agreed. "This was Zhao's

doing. He still wants to capture the Avatar first to impress your father, so he blew up your ship to eliminate the competition."

Uncle looked past me and pointed out toward what was left of my ship. "And here he comes now to view his handiwork."

I spotted Zhao's massive warship in the distance.

"You must hide, Prince Zuko," Uncle said, getting to his feet. "It is better that he thinks you are dead."

Uncle was right. As much as I would have loved to confront Zhao, I stood no chance against him and all his soldiers. I slipped into the bushes and waited.

A little while later, Zhao came ashore.

"General Iroh, I was nearby and saw the explosion," Zhao said, his voice filled with false concern. "I am relieved to see you alive."

Every impulse told me to attack from my hiding place and strike him down. But I forced myself to keep my rage in check.

"Thank you, Commander," Uncle said. "Unfortunately, my nephew was not as lucky."

"I am deeply sorry, General, for your loss," Zhao said, again not sounding the least bit sincere. But I could not believe that he was convinced that

I had died! I had no idea my uncle could lie so well.

Then Zhao extended a surprising invitation to my uncle. "I would be honored if you would join me on my historic journey to the Northern Water Tribe stronghold," he said. "There, I will wipe out all remaining opposition to the Fire Nation and put an end to this war."

"The honor would be all mine, Commander," Uncle said, bowing slightly. "Allow me to gather a few things first."

"By all means," Zhao said. "I will see you on board."

"Oh, can you spare one of your guards to help an old man carry his belongings?" Uncle asked.

Wait—what did Uncle just say? What was he thinking?

"Of course," Zhao replied. Then he ordered one of his guards to help Uncle.

Once Zhao had returned to his ship, Uncle asked the guard to help him carry something heavy. "It is right this way," Uncle said, leading the guard toward the bushes where I hid.

Then I understood. As the guard stepped around the bushes, I pulled a blast of flame from the embers of Uncle's campfire, and knocked the guard to the ground. He lay there unconscious.

"Well done, Zuko," Uncle said. "Now, quickly. Slip into his uniform. You will escort me onto Zhao's ship. And he will provide passage for us both."

I put on the guard's Fire Nation uniform, careful to hide my face beneath the helmet. Then, carrying Uncle's belongings, I followed him onto Zhao's ship. Once on board, I hid in a storage room for the long journey. Uncle snuck food to me as the dreary, tedious days slowly passed.

Then, one day, about a week after we had come aboard, Uncle returned to the storage room following a meeting with Zhao up on deck.

"Any problems?" I asked, as Uncle closed the door behind him.

"We have arrived at the Northern Water Tribe stronghold," he explained. "They believe the boy is there."

"Why do you seem upset then?" I asked. "Zhao is bringing us right to the Avatar."

"Zhao has no sacredness," Uncle said sharply. "He is cold-blooded and insincere. Zuko, are you sure you want to be here?"

Why, after all we have been through, does he still not understand?

"I will not be allowed to live in peace until I bring the Avatar to my father," I said through clenched teeth. "Is that still not clear to you?"

Uncle sighed deeply. "Very well," he said. "Then we should plan our next steps."

"I have had nothing but time to plan on this voyage," I said. "I have an idea. I am ready to capture the Avatar before Zhao even docks his ship."

CHAPTER 10

I stood at the rear of the ship gazing out at the frozen sea. The surface of the ocean was a shiny sheet of ice with a few small breaks where I could see water. I wondered for a moment if my plan would work, if I could survive for long under all that ice. Then I shrugged off any doubts. I would reach the Avatar before Zhao.

"Be sure to keep your uniform closed up to your neck," said Uncle, who stood beside me.

I nodded and secured the top button.

"And remember, your own chi, your own fire-bending ability, can warm you," Uncle added.

"I will remember," I said as I lowered myself into a boat. I took a deep breath and began to paddle toward the shore.

"Zuko," Uncle called out, his voice cracking with emotion. "You have always been like a son to me."

I looked back at him. "I know, Uncle," I said with a smile. And I think he knew that I felt the same way about him.

"Be sure to keep your head covered to stay warm. And remember to change your wet clothes when you get out of the water," Uncle added, though his voice grew faint the farther I paddled.

"Okay, Uncle," I shouted back.

When I had run out of breaks in the ice to paddle through, I began to breathe deeply and concentrate on the firebending energy within me. I leaned over the edge of the boat.

Well, this was it: time to jump. No turning back once I leaped off. I would capture the Avatar or perish trying. Then without another thought, I dove from the boat and plunged into the icy water.

The chill of freezing water gripped my body. My skin began to tingle, then went numb. Glancing up, I saw the bottom of an endless sheet of ice above me. I could see no obvious way back up. Ahead, I saw only darkness. I felt uncontrollable panic rise up inside me as I forced myself to continue swimming forward.

What have I done? I'm going to run out of air any minute! I'm going to drown, if I don't freeze first.

My chest burned from the lack of air. I could barely feel my hands and feet. Then I remembered Uncle's words: *Your own firebending ability can warm you.*

I quickly swam up toward the surface. Forcing my racing mind to calm down, I placed the palms of both my hands onto the underside of the ice. Focusing my firebending energy up into my hands, I felt them begin to warm. Within seconds they were glowing bright red, radiating heat.

Just as I felt like I was about to pass out, like my lungs were about to burst, my glowing hands began melting the ice and I started rising up. I felt the top of the ice crack and looked up to see a circle of water opening directly above me. My hands broke the surface, followed by my head. I was out. I was free. I gulped greedily, filling my lungs with sweet, cool air.

Pulling myself up and out of the water, I rolled onto my back and took several more deep breaths.

When I climbed to my feet, I saw that I was in someone's home. I had made it! I was inside the Northern
Water Tribe stronghold.

Loud warning bells began to ring outside. Looking out the window, I saw people running and
screaming. Zhao's ship must have just landed. His
invasion had begun. I couldn't afford to waste any
time. I slipped from the home and ran out into the
panicking crowd.

This truly was a city of ice. The buildings were
shaped from ice, no doubt created by the last
remaining waterbenders who lived here.

When I reached the stronghold's main courtyard, I
stopped in my tracks. There was the Avatar, along with

the girl from the Southern Water Tribe who traveled with him. It seemed that my luck was about to improve.

Keeping to the shadows, I followed them out of the courtyard and toward the back of the city. There, the ice buildings stopped at the foot of a towering mountain. I watched as the Avatar and the girl started up a steep stairway that led through a gap in the mountain. Torches lined the stairway's stone walls. I grabbed one and followed.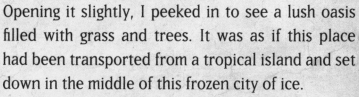

At the top of the stairs I reached an old wooden door. Opening it slightly, I peeked in to see a lush oasis filled with grass and trees. It was as if this place had been transported from a tropical island and set down in the middle of this frozen city of ice.

I spotted the Avatar sitting next to a small pond beside a flowing stream. He appeared to be in some kind of trance. The girl stood beside him and spoke softly.

"I knew you were real," she said to him. "I always knew you would return."

I threw the door open and stepped into this

grassy place. "Me too," I said. "I knew he was real. And I knew he was alive."

The girl turned to look at me, shock and anger on her face.

"The Fire Lord's son!" she cried. "You took him from our village. Aang said you tried to take him from the Fire Nation at the Northern Air Temple. I won't let you take him from here."

Ah, the Avatar's name is Aang. . . .

I dropped the burning torch, then stepped forward in a firebending move that sent flames from the torch shooting right at the girl.

Showing no fear, she reacted swiftly and confidently. Whipping her arms forward, she pulled water from the rushing stream that leaped up and met my fire, extinguishing the flames.

She is a waterbender!

Yet she is from the Southern Water Tribe. I thought all the waterbenders were here, in the north.

I directed another blast of fire right at her, but again she met my attack with a wave of water. The two elements met in midair, dissolving into steam. It was quite an impressive display.

"Who are you?" I asked.

"My name is Katara," she said proudly, her eyes never leaving mine. "I am the only waterbender left in the Southern Water Tribe."

She is a skilled adversary, worthy of respect. But nothing will stop me in my quest. I lifted both my arms and sent two bursts of flame racing at her, one from each side.

Katara turned and stopped one flame with a rush of water, then turned toward the second flame just as it struck her down. She lay sprawled on the grass, unconscious.

Quickly, I grabbed the Avatar, who remained in his deep trance. Slinging him over my shoulder, I looked down at Katara.

"I'm not allowed to go home without him," I said. "I need him to regain my honor." Then I ran for the stairs, carrying my prize.

CHAPTER 11

Hurrying back through the city, I slipped into a storage room in a corner of the stronghold. I leaned the Avatar against a wall since he remained in his trance.

I could hear the sounds of battle between Zhao's Fire Nation soldiers and the people of the Northern Water Tribe coming from outside—explosions, people screaming and barking orders.

"We'll just wait until everyone's fighting everyone," I said to the sleeping boy. "Then in the night, we'll slip out and make for the Fire Nation . . . and the end of my exile."

I watched as he breathed calmly, his eyes flicker-
ing back and forth beneath his closed eyelids. "That
must be some dream you're having," I said.

I cannot believe that I finally have him. He looks
like the meekest of children, for one with such great
power. Hard to believe that this boy is the Avatar.

"I have to bring you back to my father," I said to
him, even though he could not hear me. "He'll be
proud. He's never been proud of me. My sister, Azula,
was always the special one. She was a firebending
prodigy, and my father loves her. He can't even look
at me sometimes. He says I'm like my mother."

The Avatar started to stir. He groaned, opened
his eyes, then climbed to his feet. Seeing me, he

slipped behind some barrels in the storeroom.

"Don't move, airbender," I shouted, standing, ready for battle.

Suddenly he jumped onto a barrel, leaped to another, then disappeared across the room. More airbending trickery, but I was ready this time.

I directed fire from a nearby torch at the spot where I had seen him vanish. As if anticipating the move, the Avatar bounced off a barrel and right up the wall. I blasted again, but the flames just missed him.

I scanned the room, but sensed that he was right behind me. Spinning, I launched a firebending blast that set the barrels near the doorway on fire. His way out was now blocked. His airbending tricks would do him no good. He was trapped, and he was mine.

Suddenly all the barrels in the room began to shake. The tops flew off a group of barrels in the center of the room and water streamed out from each one, rushing toward me. Before I could move, I was surrounded by water, which instantly turned to ice.

I was trapped!

Standing in the doorway was Katara. I watched as she gracefully completed the waterbending move that locked me in this ice prison. Even my head was surrounded, but I could still breathe since she left a small bubble of air around my face.

"Are you okay?" she asked the Avatar, hugging him tightly. He nodded. "Did the spirits tell you anything during your time in the spirit world?"

Spirit world? So that's what that trance was. The Avatar was in touch with the spirit world. Uncle had said he could do that.

"Yes," the boy replied. "But I'm still not sure what to do."

I felt my body temperature start to drop. And I was running out of air.

"Let's go," Katara said.

The Avatar followed her, but just before stepping through the doorway he turned back toward me. Pulling his hands to his waist, he executed a waterbending move of his own, melting the ice around my head. The water splashed away and I gasped for breath, taking in big gulps of air. I began to shiver uncontrollably.

"You won't be killed by the waterbenders if you stay hidden here," he said.

I was surprised. Why did he care whether I lived or died?

"It was fun escaping with you from the Air Temple," the boy continued. "We could be friends, you know." Then he turned and left the room.

Friends? With the Avatar? He understands nothing about me.

My hands began to go numb. I felt myself slipping into darkness. Then, as I had done under the icy ocean, I focused my last bit of firebending energy into my hands. It took longer this time, but eventually they began to heat up and glow. Soon the ice started to melt and I was free.

Rushing from the storage room, I soon came to a bridge. Commander Zhao stood in the center of the span.

Well, if I couldn't have the Avatar, at least I could take my revenge on Zhao.

When I stepped out onto the bridge, Zhao's face turned pale. That was priceless.

"I killed you!" he shouted.

Before I could speak or move, Uncle appeared, hurrying to my side. Behind him, a troop of waterbenders rushed toward us.

"Come away from him, Nephew," Uncle shouted. "There are too many soldiers now. They will never let you take the Avatar. We must leave immediately."

I stared at Zhao. This could not be true. Would my revenge on Zhao also be denied? Would I be a total failure?

"Zuko, he wants you to fight so he can capture you," Uncle said. "Walk away. It is your only choice."

As hard as it was for me to accept, I knew Uncle was right. If I fought, I would certainly be captured by Zhao's soldiers or by the waterbenders, and my quest would be finished. I had to leave now and come up with a new plan—again.

I turned away from Zhao and immediately heard the sound of fire crackling through the air, rushing toward me. Uncle quickly stepped around me, placing himself between me and the fire blast. He extended his hands and directed the fire away from us.

"You stand alone, Zhao," Uncle shouted, "and that has always been your great mistake."

Then Uncle and I ran from the bridge. I glanced back over my shoulder to see the waterbenders arriving. They surrounded Zhao with streams of water until his limp, lifeless form collapsed to the ground.

Reaching the shoreline, Uncle and I took a Water Tribe kayak, and paddled out into the ocean. When we were some distance from the stronghold, I stared in disbelief at the sight of the ocean rising in a great wall of water.

I saw the Avatar standing on the outer wall of the stronghold. His tattoos were glowing, and his arms were raised. *He* was controlling the massive tower of water!

"The Avatar has mastered waterbending," Uncle

observed as we paddled away. The Fire Nation fleet was also retreating. "He will be more difficult to capture now."

"We must still try," I replied. "*I* must. You have said that is my destiny. And it remains the only way I can regain my honor."

You have not seen the last of me, Avatar.